Ceana Has CP

WRITTEN BY
C. Fran Card

ILLUSTRATED BY
Violet Freeland

This book is dedicated to my 9 grandchildren:
Taylor, Alexis, KC, Ben, Cullen, Nicole, Ali, Samantha
and especially Ceana, whose life provided the
inspiration for this book. Thank you all for your love.

Ceana and her big brother, Cullen,
live in a house way up on a hill.

You have to go up, **up, up** a long, long driveway to get to the house.

Ceana and Cullen live with their mom
and dad. Ceana's dad teaches school.
He leaves early in the morning.
He always takes his briefcase.

Cullen goes to school in the afternoon.
Ceana and her mom walk Cullen down the
long, long driveway to wait for the bus.

Ceana, Cullen and their mom wait on the bench Ceana's dad built.
Ceana and Cullen play a game called, "Who can see the bus first?"
The first one to yell, **"Bus! Bus!"** is the winner.

Ceana doesn't walk the same as her mom,
dad and Cullen, because Ceana has CP.
CP is a short way to say Cerebral Palsy. CP means that
kids who have it can't move some of their muscles the
way other kids do. Most kids with CP are not very strong.
CP doesn't let the muscles in Ceana's left leg do what
she wants it to do. When she walks, she swings
her left leg out, and then it plops down.

When you have CP, you may have to use crutches, a walker or ride in a wheelchair. Some kids who have CP have trouble talking.

Ceana can talk and walk and run. She can't run as fast as she wants to, or hang from the monkey bars, because Ceana has CP.

Ceana loves to run and chase. She likes chasing Cullen.
She loves to run after her grandma's hairless cats.

The cats let her catch them because they love Ceana.
She hugs them, kisses them and holds them very gently.
She loves to give them treats.

While Cullen and his dad are at school, Ceana and her mom have time for fun. Sometimes they make cookies. Ceana stands on a stool so she can stir the cookie dough. It's a hard job for a little girl.

Ceana and her mom use an ice cream scoop so each cookie
is round and the same size. Ceana makes two really
BIG cookies, one for her and one for Cullen.

When Cullen gets home from school, he and Ceana eat their really **BIG** cookies. They like to dunk them in **BIG** glasses of milk.

Now it's time for Ceana to do her exercises.
Ceana's mom helps Ceana stretch the
muscles in her foot and leg every day.

Push and hold. Push and hold. They do the
exercises every day because Ceana has CP.

Ceana will do her stretching exercises
every day even when she is big
because CP never goes away.

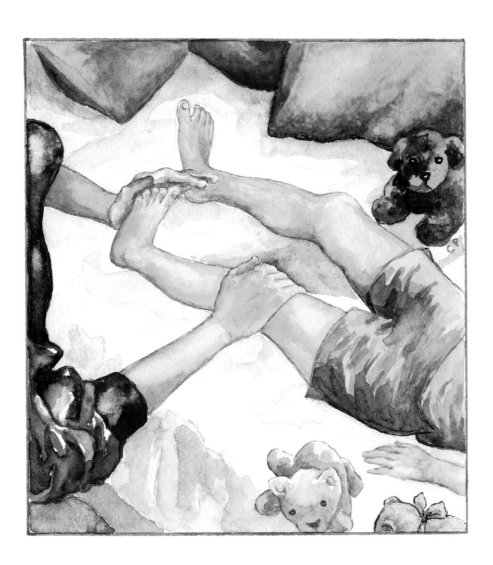

CP doesn't hurt.
Remember, CP is a
short way of saying
Cerebral Palsy.

Ceana has her own bedroom where she hides her treasures.
Her favorite hiding place is in a blue box, way back in her closet.

She has some gum, some pennies and some stickers hidden in her special place. Only Ceana, and now you, know about her secret hiding place.

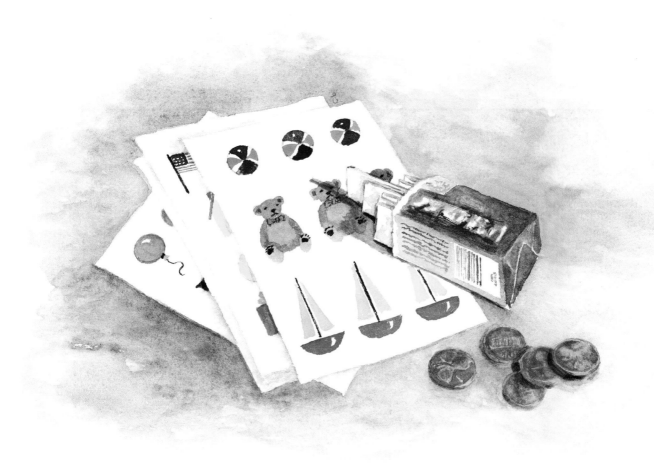

Ceana loves to tease her big brother Cullen.
Sometimes she takes his favorite truck and hides it in her secret hiding place.
Do you remember where that is?

Sometimes Ceana and Cullen get a special treat from their dad.
When he comes home from teaching, he takes them for a long ride on his
BIG ORANGE TRACTOR.

Ceana loves to read to her baby dolls. Her favorite baby is Ella.
She reads lots of books to them and they **always** listen.

Ceana is a happy little girl with a **BIG** smile.
She would love to be your friend.

Ceana has CP.

P.S. — Did you find the letters "CP" hidden on each page?

Until next time,
Goodbye!